WAYFARERS ALL

from THE WIND IN THE WILLOWS by KENNETH GRAHAME

illustrated by Beverley Gooding

Charles Scribner's Sons · New York

1 3 5 7 9 11 13 15 17 19 XD/C 20 18 16 14 12 10 8 6 4 2

Printed in England

Library of Congress Catalog Card Number   80—9054
ISBN   0–684–16876–6

THE Water Rat was restless, and he did not exactly know why. To all appearances the summer's pomp was still at fullest height, and although in the tilled acres green had given way to gold, though rowans were reddening, and the woods were dashed here and there with a tawny fierceness, yet light and warmth and colour were still present in undiminished measure, clean of any chilly premonitions of the passing year. But the constant chorus of the orchards and hedges had shrunk to a casual evensong from a few yet unwearied performers; the robin was beginning to assert himself once more; and there was a feeling in the air of change and departure. The cuckoo, of course, had long been silent; but many another feathered friend, for months a part of the familiar landscape and its small society, was missing too, and it seemed that the ranks thinned steadily day by day. Rat, ever observant of all winged movement, saw that it was taking daily a southing tendency; and even as he lay in bed at night he thought he could make out, passing in the darkness overhead, the beat and quiver of impatient pinions, obedient to the peremptory call.

3

Nature's Grand Hotel has its Season, like the others. As the guests one by one pack, pay, and depart, and the seats at the *table-d'hôte* shrink pitifully at each succeeding meal; as suites of rooms are closed, carpets taken up, and waiters sent away; those boarders who are staying on, *en pension*, until the next year's full reopening, cannot help being somewhat affected by all these flittings and farewells, this eager discussion of plans, routes, and fresh quarters, this daily shrinkage in the stream of comradeship. One gets unsettled, depressed, and inclined to be querulous. Why this craving for change? Why not stay on quietly here, like us, and be jolly? You don't know this hotel out of the season, and what fun we have among ourselves, we fellows who remain and see the whole interesting year out. All very true, no doubt, the others always reply; we quite envy you – and some other year perhaps – but just now we have engagements – and there's the bus at the door – our time is up! So they depart, with a smile and a nod, and we miss them, and feel resentful. The Rat was a self-sufficing sort of animal, rooted to the land, and, whoever went, he stayed; still, he could not help noticing what was in the air, and feeling some of its influence in his bones.

It was difficult to settle down to anything seriously, with all this flitting going on. Leaving the water-side, where rushes stood thick and tall in a stream that was becoming sluggish and low, he wandered country-wards, crossed a field or two of pasturage already looking dusty and parched, and thrust into the great realm of wheat, yellow, wavy, and murmurous, full of quiet motion and small whisperings. Here he often

4

loved to wander, through the forest of stiff strong stalks that
carried their own golden sky away over his head – a sky that
was always dancing, shimmering, softly talking; or swaying
strongly to the passing wind and recovering itself with a toss
and a merry laugh. Here, too, he had many small friends, a
society complete in itself, leading full and busy lives, but
always with a spare moment to gossip and exchange news
with a visitor. To-day, however, though they were civil

enough, the field-mice and harvest-mice seemed pre-occupied. Many were digging and tunnelling busily; others, gathered together in small groups, examined plans and drawings of small flats, stated to be desirable and compact, and situated conveniently near the Stores. Some were hauling out dusty trunks and dress-baskets, others were already elbow-deep packing their belongings; while everywhere piles and bundles of wheat, oats, barley, beech-mast and nuts, lay about ready for transport.

'Here's old Ratty!' they cried as soon as they saw him. 'Come and bear a hand, Rat, and don't stand about idle!'

'What sort of games are you up to?' said the Water Rat severely. 'You know it isn't time to be thinking of winter quarters yet, by a long way!'

'O yes, we know that,' explained a field-mouse rather shamefacedly; 'but it's always as well to be in good time, isn't it? We really *must* get all the furniture and baggage and stores moved out of this before those horrid machines begin clicking round the fields; and then, you know, the best flats get picked up so quickly nowadays, and if you're late you have to put up with *anything*; and they want such a lot of doing up, too, before they're fit to move into. Of course, we're early, we know that; but we're only just making a start.'

'O, bother *starts*,' said the Rat. 'It's a splendid day. Come for a row, or a stroll along the hedges, or a picnic in the woods, or something.'

'Well, I *think* not *to-day*, thank you,' replied the field-mouse hurriedly. 'Perhaps some *other* day – when we've more *time* —'

The Rat, with a snort of contempt, swung round to go, tripped over a hat-box, and fell, with undignified remarks.

'If people would be more careful,' said a field-mouse rather stiffly, 'and look where they're going, people wouldn't hurt themselves – and forget themselves. Mind that hold-all, Rat! You'd better sit down somewhere. In an hour or two we may be more free to attend to you.'

'You won't be "free," as you call it, much this side of Christmas, I can see that,' retorted the Rat grumpily, as he picked his way out of the field.

He returned somewhat despondently to his river again – his faithful, steady-going old river, which never packed up, flitted, or went into winter quarters.

In the osiers which fringed the bank he spied a swallow sitting. Presently it was joined by another, and then by a third; and the birds, fidgeting restlessly on their bough, talked together earnestly and low.

'What, *already*?' said the Rat, strolling up to them. 'What's the hurry? I call it simply ridiculous.'

'O, we're not off yet, if that's what you mean,' replied the first swallow. 'We're only making plans and arranging things. Talking it over, you know – what route we're taking this year, and where we'll stop, and so on. That's half the fun!'

'Fun?' said the Rat; 'now that's just what I don't understand. If you've *got* to leave this pleasant place, and your friends who will miss you, and your snug homes that you've just settled into, why, when the hour strikes I've no doubt you'll go bravely, and face all the trouble and discomfort and change and newness, and make believe that you're not very unhappy. But to want to talk about it, or even think about it, till you really need—'

'No, you don't understand, naturally,' said the second swallow. 'First, we feel it stirring within us, a sweet unrest; then back come the recollections one by one, like homing pigeons. They flutter through our dreams at night, they fly with us in

8

our wheelings and circlings by day. We hunger to inquire of each other, to compare notes and assure ourselves that it was all really true, as one by one the scents and sounds and names of long-forgotten places come gradually back and beckon to us.'

'Couldn't you stop on for just this year?' suggested the Water Rat wistfully. 'We'll all do our best to make you feel at home. You've no idea what good times we have here, while you are far away.'

'I tried "stopping on" one year,' said the third swallow. 'I had grown so fond of the place that when the time came I hung back and let the others go on without me. For a few weeks it was all well enough, but afterwards, O the weary length of the nights! The shivering, sunless days! The air so clammy and chill, and not an insect in an acre of it! No, it was no good; my courage broke down, and one cold, stormy night I took wing, flying well inland on account of the strong easterly gales. It was snowing hard as I beat through the passes of the great mountains, and I had a stiff fight to win through; but never shall I forget the blissful feeling of the hot sun again on my back as I sped down to the lakes that lay so blue and placid below me, and the taste of my first fat insect! The past was like a bad dream; the future was all happy holiday as I moved southwards week by week, easily, lazily, lingering as long as I dared, but always heeding the call! No, I had had my warning; never again did I think of disobedience.'

'Ah, yes, the call of the South, of the South!' twittered the other two dreamily. 'Its songs, its hues, its radiant air! O, do you remember—' and, forgetting the Rat, they slid into passionate reminiscence, while he listened fascinated, and his heart burned within him. In himself, too, he knew that it was vibrating at last, that chord hitherto dormant and unsuspected. The mere chatter of these southern-bound birds, their pale and second-hand reports, had yet power to awaken this wild new sensation and thrill him through and through with it; what would one moment of the real thing work in him – one passionate touch of the real southern sun, one waft of the authentic odour? With closed eyes he dared to dream a moment in full abandonment, and when he looked again the river seemed steely and chill, the green fields grey and lightless. Then his loyal heart seemed to cry out on his weaker self for its treachery.

'Why do you ever come back, then, at all?' he demanded of the swallows jealously. 'What do you find to attract you in this poor drab little country?'

'And do you think,' said the first swallow, 'that the other call is not for us too, in its due season? The call of lush meadow-grass, wet orchards, warm, insect-haunted ponds, of browsing cattle, of haymaking, and all the farm-buildings clustering round the House of the perfect Eaves?'

'Do you suppose,' asked the second one, 'that you are the only living thing that craves with a hungry longing to hear the cuckoo's note again?'

'In due time,' said the third, 'we shall be homesick once more for quiet water-lilies swaying on the surface of an English stream. But to-day all that seems pale and thin and very far away. Just now our blood dances to other music.'

They fell a-twittering among themselves once more, and this time their intoxicating babble was of violet seas, tawny sands, and lizard-haunted walls.

Restlessly the Rat wandered off once more, climbed the slope that rose gently from the north bank of the river, and lay looking out towards the great ring of Downs that barred his vision further southwards – his simple horizon hitherto, his Mountains of the Moon, his limit behind which lay nothing he had cared to see or to know. To-day, to him gazing south with a new-born need stirring in his heart, the clear sky over their long low outline seemed to pulsate with promise; to-day, the unseen was everything, the unknown the only real fact of life. On this side of the hills was now the real blank, on the other lay the crowded and coloured panorama that his inner eye was seeing so clearly. What seas lay beyond, green, leaping, and crested! What sun-bathed coasts, along which the white villas glittered against the olive woods! What quiet harbours, thronged with gallant shipping bound for purple islands of wine and spice, islands set low in languorous waters!

He rose and descended river-wards once more; then changed his mind and sought the side of the dusty lane. There, laying half-buried in the thick, cool under-hedge tangle that bordered it, he could muse on the metalled road

and all the wondrous world that it led to; on all the wayfarers, too, that might have trodden it, and the fortunes and adventures they had gone to seek or found unseeking – out there, beyond – beyond!

Footsteps fell on his ear, and the figure of one that walked somewhat wearily came into view; and he saw that it was a Rat, and a very dusty one. The wayfarer, as he reached him, saluted with a gesture of courtesy that had something foreign about it – hesitated a moment – then with a pleasant smile turned from the track and sat down by his side in the cool herbage. He seemed tired, and the Rat let him rest unquestioned, understanding something of what was in his thoughts; knowing, too, the value all animals attach at times to mere silent companionship, when the weary muscles slacken and the mind marks time.

The wayfarer was lean and keen-featured, and somewhat bowed at the shoulders; his paws were thin and long, his eyes much wrinkled at the corners, and he wore small gold earrings in his neatly-set, well-shaped ears. His knitted jersey was of a faded blue, his breeches, patched and stained, were based on a blue foundation, and his small belongings that he carried were tied up in a blue cotton handkerchief.

When he had rested awhile the stranger sighed, snuffed the air, and looked about him.

'That was clover, that warm whiff on the breeze,' he remarked; 'and those are cows we hear cropping the grass behind us and blowing softly between mouthfuls. There is a sound of distant reapers, and yonder rises a blue line of cottage smoke against the woodland. The river runs some-where close by, for I hear the call of a moorhen, and I see by your build that you're a fresh-water mariner. Everything seems asleep, and yet going on all the time. It is a goodly life that you lead, friend; no doubt the best in the world, if only you are strong enough to lead it!'

'Yes, it's *the* life, the only life, to live,' responded the Water Rat dreamily, and without his usual whole-hearted convic-tion.

'I did not say exactly that,' replied the stranger cautiously; 'but no doubt it's the best. I've tried it, and I know. And because I've just tried it – six months of it – and know it's the best, here am I, footsore and hungry, tramping away from it, tramping southward, following the old call, back to the old life, *the* life which is mine and which will not let me go.

'Is this, then, yet another of them?' mused the Rat. 'And where have you just come from?' he asked. He hardly dared to ask where he was bound for; he seemed to know the answer only too well.

'Nice little farm,' replied the wayfarer briefly. 'Upalong in that direction' – he nodded northwards. 'Never mind about it. I had everything I could want – everything I had any right to expect of life, and more; and here I am! Glad to be here all the same, though, glad to be here! So many miles farther on the road, so many hours nearer to my heart's desire!'

His shining eyes held fast to the horizon, and he seemed to be listening for some sound that was wanting from that inland acreage, vocal as it was with the cheerful music of pasturage and farmyard.

'You are not one of *us*,' said the Water Rat, 'nor yet a farmer; nor even, I should judge, of this country.'

'Right,' replied the stranger. 'I'm a seafaring rat, I am, and the port I originally hail from is Constantinople, though I'm a sort of a foreigner there too, in a manner of speaking. You will have heard of Constantinople, friend? A fair city, and an ancient and glorious one. And you may have heard, too, of Sigurd, King of Norway, and how he sailed thither with sixty ships, and how he and his men rode up through streets all canopied in their honour with purple and gold; and how the Emperor and Empress came down and banqueted with him on board his ship. When Sigurd returned home, many of his Northmen remained behind and entered the Emperor's body-guard, and my ancestor, a Norwegian born, stayed behind too, with the ships that Sigurd gave the Emperor. Seafarers we have ever been, and no wonder; as for me, the city of my birth is no more my home than any pleasant port between there and the London River. I know them all, and they know me. Set me down on any of their quays or foreshores, and I am home again.'

'I suppose you go great voyages,' said the Water Rat with

growing interest. 'Months and months out of sight of land, and provisions running short, and allowanced as to water, and your mind communing with the mighty ocean, and all that sort of thing?'

'By no means,' said the Sea Rat frankly. 'Such a life as you describe would not suit me at all. I'm in the coasting trade, and rarely out of sight of land. It's the jolly times on shore that appeal to me, as much as any seafaring. O, those southern seaports! The smell of them, the riding-lights at night, the glamour!'

'Well, perhaps you have chosen the better way,' said the Water Rat, but rather doubtfully. 'Tell me something of your coasting, then, if you have a mind to, and what sort of harvest an animal of spirit might hope to bring home from it to warm his latter days with gallant memories by the fireside; for my life, I confess to you, feels to me to-day somewhat narrow and circumscribed.'

'My last voyage,' began the Sea Rat, 'that landed me eventually in this country, bound with high hopes for my inland farm, will serve as a good example of any of them, and, indeed, as an epitome of my highly-coloured life. Family troubles, as usual, began it. The domestic storm-cone was hoisted, and I shipped myself on board a small trading vessel bound from Constantinople, by classic seas whose every wave throbs with a deathless memory, to the Grecian Islands and the Levant. Those were golden days and balmy nights! In and out of harbour all the time – old friends everywhere – sleeping in some cool temple or ruined cistern during the heat of the day – feasting and song after sundown, under great stars set in a velvet sky! Thence we turned and coasted up the Adriatic, its shores swimming in an atmosphere of amber, rose, and aquamarine; we lay in wide land-locked harbours, we roamed through ancient and noble cities, until at last one morning, as the sun rose royally behind us, we rode into Venice down a path of gold. O, Venice is a fine city, wherein a rat can wander at his ease and take his pleasure! Or, when weary of wandering, can sit at the edge of the Grand Canal at night, feasting with his friends, when the air is full of music and the sky full of stars, and the lights flash and shimmer on the polished steel prows of the swaying gondolas, packed so that you could walk across the canal on them from side to side! And then the food – do you like shell-fish? Well, well, we won't linger over that now.'

He was silent for a time; and the Water Rat, silent too and enthralled, floated on dream-canals and heard a phantom song pealing high between vaporous grey wave-lapped walls.

'Southward we sailed again at last,' continued the Sea Rat, 'coasting down the Italian shore, till finally we made Palermo, and there I quitted for a long, happy spell on shore. I never stick too long to one ship; one gets narrow-minded and pre-judiced. Besides, Sicily is one of my happy hunting-grounds. I know everybody there, and their ways just suit me. I spent many jolly weeks in the island, staying with friends up country. When I grew restless again I took advantage of a ship that was trading to Sardinia and Corsica; and very glad I was to feel the fresh breeze and the sea-spray in my face once more.'

'But isn't it very hot and stuffy, down in the – hold, I think you call it?' asked the Water Rat.

The seafarer looked at him with the suspicion of a wink. 'I'm an old hand,' he remarked with much simplicity. 'The cap-tain's cabin's good enough for me.'

'It's a hard life, by all accounts,' murmured the Rat, sunk in deep thought.

'For the crew it is,' replied the seafarer gravely, again with the ghost of a wink.

'From Corsica,' he went on, 'I made use of a ship that was taking wine to the mainland. We made Alassio in the evening, lay to, hauled up our wine-casks, and hove them overboard, tied one to the other by a long line. Then the crew took to the boats and rowed shorewards, singing as they went, and draw-ing after them the long bobbing procession of casks, like a mile of porpoises. On the sands they had horses waiting, which dragged the casks up the steep street of the little town with a fine rush and clatter and scramble. When the last cask was in, we went and refreshed and rested, and sat late into the night, drinking with our friends; and next morning I was off to the great olive-woods for a spell and a rest. For now I had done with islands for the time, and ports and shipping were plentiful; so I led a lazy life among the peasants, lying and watching them work, or stretched high on the hillside with the blue Mediterranean far below me. And so at length, by easy stages, and partly on foot, partly by sea, to Marseilles, and the meeting of old shipmates, and the visiting of great ocean-bound vessels, and feasting once more. Talk of shell-fish! Why, sometimes I dream of the shell-fish of Marseilles, and wake up crying!'

'That reminds me,' said the polite Water Rat; 'you happened to mention that you were hungry, and I ought to have spoken earlier. Of course you will stop and take your midday meal with me? My hole is close by; it is some time past noon, and you are very welcome to whatever there is.'

'Now I call that kind and brotherly of you,' said the Sea Rat. 'I was indeed hungry when I sat down, and ever since I inadvertently happened to mention shell-fish, my pangs have been extreme. But couldn't you fetch it along out here? I am none too fond of going under hatches, unless I'm obliged to; and then, while we eat, I could tell you more concerning my voyages and the pleasant life I lead – at least, it is very pleasant to me, and by your attention I judge it commends itself to you; whereas if we go indoors it is a hundred to one that I shall presently fall asleep.'

'That is indeed an excellent suggestion,' said the Water Rat, and hurried off home. There he got out the luncheon-basket and packed a simple meal, in which, remembering the stranger's origin and preferences, he took care to include a yard of long French bread, a sausage out of which the garlic sang, some cheese which lay down and cried, and a long-necked straw-covered flask containing bottled sunshine shed and garnered on far Southern slopes. Thus laden, he returned with all speed, and blushed for pleasure at the old seaman's commendations of his taste and judgment, as together they unpacked the basket and laid out the contents on the grass by the roadside.

The Sea Rat, as soon as his hunger was somewhat assuaged, continued the history of his latest voyage, conducting his simple hearer from port to port of Spain, landing him at Lisbon, Oporto, and Bordeaux, introducing him to the pleasant harbours of Cornwall and Devon, and so up the Channel to that final quayside, where, landing after winds long contrary, storm-driven and weather-beaten, he had caught the first magical hints and heraldings of another Spring and, fired by these, had sped on a long tramp inland, hungry for the experiment of life on some quiet farmstead, very far from the weary beating of any sea.

Spellbound and quivering with excitement, the Water Rat followed the Adventurer league by league, over stormy bays, through crowded roadsteads, across harbour bars on a racing tide, up winding rivers that hid their busy little towns round a sudden turn; and left him with a regretful sigh planted at his dull inland farm, about which he desired to hear nothing.

By this time the meal was over, and the Seafarer, refreshed and strengthened, his voice more vibrant, his eye lit with a brightness that seemed caught from some far-away sea-beacon, filled his glass with the red and glowing vintage of the South, and, leaning towards the Water Rat, compelled his gaze and held him, body and soul, while he talked. Those eyes were of the changing foam-streaked grey-green of leaping

24

Northern seas; in the glass shone a hot ruby that seemed the very heart of the South, beating for him who had courage to respond to its pulsation. The twin lights, the shifting grey and the steadfast red, mastered the Water Rat and held him bound, fascinated, powerless. The quiet world outside their rays receded far away and ceased to be. And the talk, the wonderful talk flowed on – or was it speech entirely, or did it pass at times into song – chanty of the sailors weighing the dripping anchor, sonorous hum of the shrouds in a tearing North-Easter, ballad of the fisherman hauling his nets at sundown against an apricot sky, chords of guitar and mandoline from gondola or caique? Did it change into the cry of the wind, plaintive at first, angrily shrill as it freshened, rising to a tearing whistle, sinking to a musical trickle of air from the leech of the bellying sail? All these sounds the spellbound listener seemed to hear, and with them the hungry complaint of the gulls and the sea-mews, the soft thunder of the breaking wave, the cry of the protesting shingle. Back into speech again it passed, and with beating heart he was following the adventures of a dozen seaports, the fights, the escapes, the rallies, the comradeships, the gallant undertakings; or he searched islands for treasure, fished in still lagoons and dozed day-long on warm white sand. Of deep-sea fishings he heard tell, and mighty silver gatherings of the mile-long net; of sudden perils, noise of breakers on a moonless night, or the tall bows of the great liner taking shape overhead through the fog; of the merry home-coming, the headland rounded, the harbour lights opened out; the groups seen dimly on the quay, the cheery hail, the splash of the hawser; the trudge up the steep little street towards the comforting glow of red-curtained windows.

Lastly, in his waking dream, it seemed to him that the Adventurer had risen to his feet, but was still speaking, still holding him fast with his sea-grey eyes.

'And now,' he was softly saying, 'I take to the road again, holding on south-westwards for many a long and dusty day; till at last, I reach the little grey sea town I know so well, that clings along one steep side of the harbour. There through dark doorways you look down flights of stone steps, overhung by great pink tufts of valerian and ending in a patch of sparkling blue water. The little boats that lie tethered to the rings and stanchions of the old sea-wall are gaily painted as those I clambered in and out of in my own childhood; the salmon leap on the flood tide, schools of mackerel flash and play past quay-sides and foreshores, and by the windows the great vessels glide, night and day, up to their moorings or forth to the open sea. There, sooner or later, the ships of all seafaring nations arrive; and there, at its destined hour, the ship of my choice will let go its anchor. I shall take my time, I shall tarry and bide, till at last the right one lies waiting for me, warped out into midstream, loaded low, her bowsprit pointing down harbour. I shall slip on board, by boat or along hawser; and

then one morning I shall wake to the song and tramp of the sailors, the clink of the capstan, and the rattle of the anchor-chain coming merrily in. We shall break out the jib and fore-sail, the white houses on the harbour side will glide slowly past us as she gathers steering-way and the voyage will have begun! As she forges towards the headland she will clothe herself with canvas; and then, once outside, the sounding slap of great green seas as she heels to the wind, pointing South!

'And you, you will come too, young brother; for the days pass, and never return, and the South still waits for you. Take the Adventure, heed the call, now ere the irrevocable moment passes! 'Tis but a banging of the door behind you, a blithesome step forward, and you are out of the old life and into the new! Then some day, some day long hence, jog home here if you will, when the cup has been drained and the play has been played, and sit down by your quiet river with a store of goodly memories for company. You can easily overtake me on the road, for you are young, and I am ageing and go softly. I will linger, and look back; and at last I will surely see you coming, eager and light-hearted, with all the South in your face!'

The voice died away and ceased, as an insect's tiny trumpet dwindles swiftly into silence; and the Water Rat, paralysed and staring, saw at last but a distant speck on the white surface of the road.

Mechanically he rose and proceeded to repack the luncheon-basket, carefully and without haste. Mechanically he returned home, gathered together a few small necessaries and special treasures he was fond of, and put them in a satchel; acting with slow deliberation, moving about the room like a sleep-walker; listening ever with parted lips. He swung the satchel over his shoulder, carefully selected a stout stick for his wayfaring, and with no haste, but with no hesitation at all, he stepped across the threshold just as the Mole appeared at the door.

'Why, where are you off to, Ratty?' asked the Mole in great surprise, grasping him by the arm.

'Going South, with the rest of them,' murmured the Rat in a dreamy monotone, never looking at him. 'Seawards first and then on shipboard, and so to the shores that are calling me!'

He pressed resolutely forward, still without haste, but with dogged fixity of purpose; but the Mole, now thoroughly alarmed, placed himself in front of him, and looking into his eyes, saw that they were glazed and set and turned a streaked and shifting grey – not his friend's eyes, but the eyes of some other animal! Grappling with him strongly he dragged him inside, threw him down, and held him.

The Rat struggled desperately for a few moments, and then his strength seemed suddenly to leave him, and he lay still and exhausted, with closed eyes, trembling. Presently the Mole assisted him to rise and placed him in a chair, where he sat collapsed and shrunken into himself, his body shaken by a violent shivering, passing in time into an hysterical fit of dry sobbing. Mole made the door fast, threw the satchel into a drawer and locked it, and sat down quietly on the table by his friend, waiting for the strange seizure to pass. Gradually the Rat sank into a troubled doze, broken by starts and confused murmurings of things strange and wild and foreign to the unenlightened Mole; and from that he passed into a deep slumber.

Very anxious in mind, the Mole left him for a time and busied himself with household matters; and it was getting dark when he returned to the parlour and found the Rat where he had left him, wide awake indeed, but listless, silent, and dejected. He took one hasty glance at his eyes; found them, to his great gratification, clear and dark and brown again as before; and then sat down and tried to cheer him up and help him to relate what had happened to him.

Poor Ratty did his best, by degrees, to explain things; but how could he put into cold words what had mostly been suggestion? How recall, for another's benefit, the haunting sea voices that had sung to him, how reproduce at second-hand the magic of the Seafarer's hundred reminiscences? Even to himself, now the spell was broken and the glamour gone, he found it difficult to account for what had seemed, some hours ago, the inevitable and only thing. It is not surprising, then, that he failed to convey to the Mole any clear idea of what he had been through that day.

To the Mole this much was plain; the fit, or attack, had passed away, and had left him sane again, though shaken and cast down by the reaction. But he seemed to have lost all interest for the time in the things that went to make up his daily life, as well as in all pleasant forecastings of the altered days and doings that the changing season was surely bringing.

Casually, then, and with seeming indifference, the Mole

turned his talk to the harvest that was being gathered in, the towering wagons and their straining teams, the growing ricks, and the large moon rising over bare acres dotted with sheaves. He talked of the reddening apples around, of the browning nuts, of jams and preserves and the distilling of cordials; till by easy stages such as these he reached mid-winter, its hearty joys and its snug home life, and then he became simply lyrical.

By degrees the Rat began to sit up and to join in. His dull eyes brightened, and he lost some of his listless air.

Presently the tactful mole slipped away and returned with a pencil and a few half-sheets of paper, which he placed on the table at his friend's elbow.

'It's quite a long time since you did any poetry,' he remarked. 'You might have a try at it this evening, instead of – well, brooding over things so much. I've an idea that you'll feel a lot better when you've got something jotted down – if it's only just the rhymes.'

The Rat pushed the paper away from him wearily, but the discreet Mole took occasion to leave the room, and when he peeped in again some time later, the Rat was absorbed and deaf to the world; alternately scribbling and sucking the top of his pencil. It is true that he sucked a good deal more than he scribbled; but it was a joy to the Mole to know that the cure had at least begun.